A BED OF YOUR OWN

by Mij Kelly

and Mary McQuillan

HODDER CHILDREN'S BOOKS

First published in Great Britain in 2011 by Hodder Children's Books
This edition published in 2018 by Hodder and Stoughton

A CIP catalogue record for this book
is available from the British Library.

ISBN 978 1 444 93925 5

Printed in China

The paper and board used in this book are from wood from responsible sources.

Hodder Children's Books
An imprint of
Hachette Children's Group
Part of Hodder and Stoughton
Carmelite House
50 Victoria Embankment
London EC4Y 0DZ

An Hachette UK Company
www.hachette.co.uk

www.hachettechildrens.co.uk

www.hachette.co.uk

To Cerys and Dylan – MK

To Finn with love – MMcQ

A BED OF YOUR OWN

MIJ
KELLY

MARY
McQUILLAN

Hodder
Children's
Books

This is the story of Suzy Sue,
ready for bed, just like you.

She brushed her teeth.
She picked up her Ted...

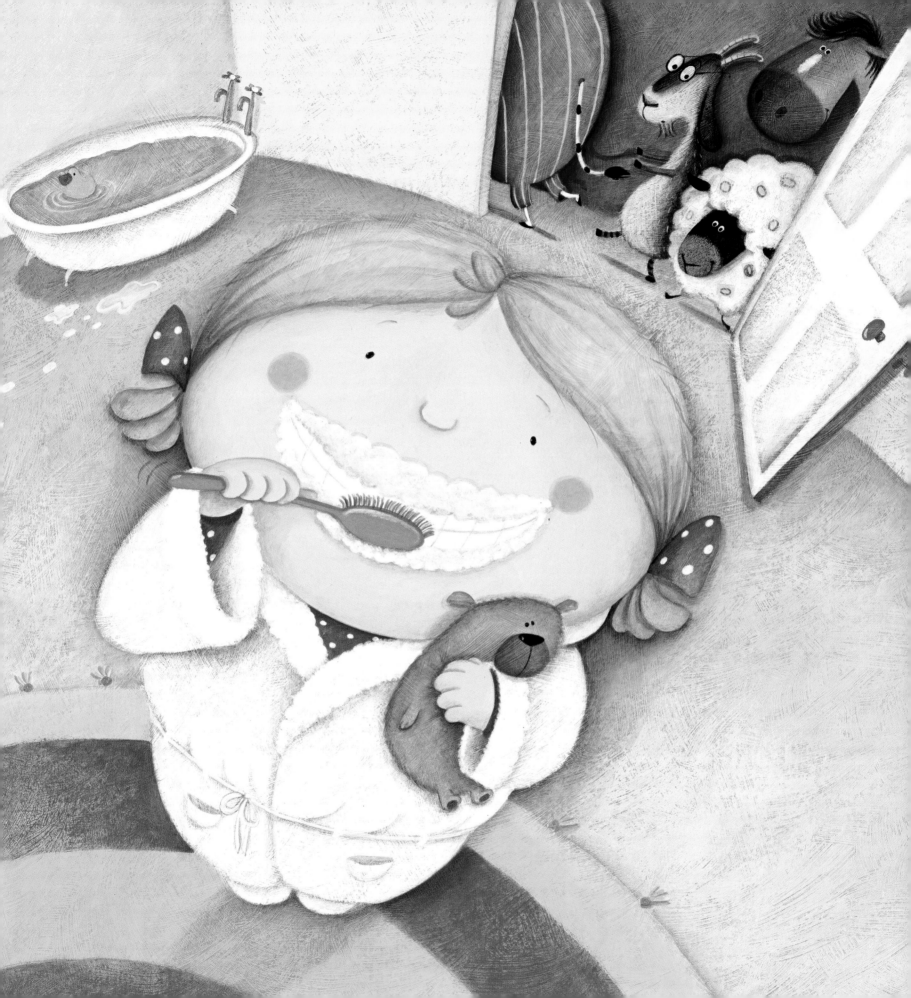

She clambered and climbed into her bed.

She yawned a huge **yawn** and turned out the light. But something somewhere wasn't quite right.

"I'm **squished**. I'm **squashed**.
I'm **uncomfy!**" she said.
"I think there's something wrong with the bed."

"I know!" said the cow.
"This bed's **far too small.**
I've tried and I've tried,
but I **can't sleep** at all."

Oh, what a **shock!**
What a **drama**
of **dramas!**

A COW in the bed – a cow in pyjamas!

"What are you doing?" said Suzy Sue.

"What do you think?"
said the cow, with a mOO.
"I'm trying to go
to sleep, of course."

"Oh, please do be quiet!"
grumbled the horse.

"How in the world can I get a nap

with the pair of you going

yappity-yap?"

Oh, what a shock! What a bolt from the blue!
A horse in the bed,
with his cuddly toys too!

And when Suzy Sue
fell back in a heap,
what she thought
was a pillow...

... was really a **sheep.**

"How can I sleep? How can I doze?

Please, please, please
leb go ob by nose!"

Oh, what a shock!

What a dreadful surprise!

But by now Suzy Sue was getting quite wise.
She threw back the covers. She called,
loud and clear,

"Are any more
animals hiding in here?"

"Just little me,"
somebody said...

... and Suzy Sue
fell out
of the bed.

Goodness gracious!
Oh, golly! Oh, gosh!

No wonder the bed was a terrible squash.
No wonder nobody could get any sleep,

with a **goat** and a **horse**
and a **COW** and a **sheep**

all tossing and turning,
all hogging the covers
and fighting for pillows and kicking
each other –

"For goodness sake!" yawned Suzy Sue.

"What on earth's got into you?

Don't you have a bed
of your OWN?"

"We can't sleep there,"
said the sheep
with a groan.

"It's too hot!" "It's too cold!"
"It's too dark!" "It's too light!"
"There's something about it that isn't quite right!"

But Suzy Sue was stern and strong.
She led them back where they belonged.

She tucked them up, and then she read
a book about going to bed.

She hugged them all and said,
"Goodnight."
But just as she went to turn down the light...

... she had an idea,
and suddenly said,
"It's all very well this going to bed,
but what really matters is

falling asleep."

"But that's the
hardest
part!" said
the sheep.

So Suzy Sue climbed in the bed.
"What you have to do," she said,
"is feel how your bed is all comfy and cosy...

... Feel how it makes you all d r o w s y and d o z y. Feel a safe, soothing softness beginning to spread from the tips of your toes to the top of your head.

And all of your worries
are wafting away,
like a bunch of
balloons on a cloudless
spring day,

and you're in a boat, floating downstream,
drifting away on a beautiful dream."

In the silence that followed, you could hear a pin drop.

"Go on," said the cow, "please don't stop."

"Oh, dear," said the goat. "Oh, dear. Oh, dear.

She's fallen asleep. But she can't sleep here!"

"She's **hogging** the bed."

"She's starting to **snore**."

"She'll keep us **awake.** It's happened before."

zzZZZZZ

"Oh, silly Suzy Sue," they said.
"Come on, let's take you back to bed.
See, each of us has our own place to rest.

The mouse has a hole.

The hen has a nest.

The pig has a sty
(it's smelly but snug).

The dog has his basket.

The cat
has her rug.

They **ALL** have beds,
and you do too.
So snuggle down, Suzy Sue."

That was the story of Suzy Sue,
safe in her own bed,

– like you should be, too!